BE KIND

Pat Zietlow Miller
Illustrated by Jen Hill

 Roaring Brook Press
New York

To two of the kindest people I know—my sister,
Pam Wells, and my friend Ellen Lawrence —P. Z. M.

To my mom and dad —J. H.

Text copyright © 2018 by Pat Zietlow Miller
Illustrations copyright © 2018 by Jen Hill
Published by Roaring Brook Press
Roaring Brook Press is a division of Holtzbrinck Publishing Holdings Limited Partnership
175 Fifth Avenue, New York, NY 10010
mackids.com

Library of Congress Control Number: 2017944499
ISBN 978-1-62672-321-4

Our books may be purchased in bulk for promotional, educational, or business use. Please contact your local bookseller or the Macmillan
Corporate and Premium Sales Department at (800) 221-7945 ext. 5442 or by e-mail at MacmillanSpecialMarkets@macmillan.com.

First edition, 2018
Printed in the United States of America by Phoenix Color, Hagerstown, Maryland
3 5 7 9 10 8 6 4

Tanisha spilled grape juice yesterday.

All
over
her
new
dress.

Everyone laughed.
I almost did, too.
But Mom always tells me
to be kind, so I tried.

I don't think it worked.
I said:

PURPLE is MY FAVORITE color.

I thought Tanisha would smile.
But she ran into the hall instead.

When she came back,
snack time was over.
She put on her art smock
and didn't look at anyone.

I almost told Tanisha that art was my favorite class, but I didn't want her to leave again.
So I painted purple splotches and added some green until I had a bunch of beautiful violets.

While I painted, I thought about Tanisha.

Should I have handed her my napkin?

Let her borrow my sweatshirt?

Spilled my juice so everyone stared at me instead?

What does it mean to be kind anyway?

Maybe it's giving.

Making cookies for Mr. Rinaldi,
who lives alone.

Letting someone with smaller feet have my too-tight shoes.

(He might win races in them, too.)

Maybe it's helping.

Putting dirty dishes in the sink.

Cleaning up after Otis,
our class guinea pig.
(He's a messy eater.)

Maybe it's paying attention.

Telling Desmond I like his blue boots.

Asking the new girl to be my partner.

Listening to Aunt Franny's stories.
(Even the ones I've heard before.)

Being kind should be easy.
Like throwing away a wrapper
or recycling a bottle.

Or saying:

THANK YOU!

BLESS YOU!

My mom says the quickest way to
be kind is to use people's names:

Hey Cayla

What's new, Omar?

Good afternoon, Rabbi Mandelbaum

Being kind can be hard, too.
Even when you know what to do.
Teaching someone something I'm good at is tricky.

(Even when I'm patient.)

And sticking up
for someone when
other kids aren't kind
is really hard.

(And really scary.)

Maybe I can't solve Tanisha's grape juice problem.
Maybe all I can do is sit by her in art class.

And paint this picture for her.
Because I know she likes purple, too.

Maybe I can only do small things.
But my small things might join small things other people do.

And, together, they could grow into something big.

Something really big.
So big that all our kindnesses spill out of our school . . .

spread throughout town . . .

travel across the country...

and go all the way...

around the world.

Right back to Tanisha and me.
So we can be kind.

Again.

WELCOME BACK!

And again.

And again.